Praise from reviewers for THE LEGEND OF SCARFACE:

"This concise and simple adaptation makes the legend readable without sacrificing any of the story's meaning or dignity. Muted full-size paintings emphasize the empathy between Scarface and his natural surroundings. The narrative gains from oral reading."   —*Language Arts*

"The twelve large full-color paintings have a dramatic strength, realistically interpreting the action, the Indian characters, and the animals." A 1978 Honor List Book.   —*Horn Book Magazine*

"Fine airbrush paintings illustrate this story of goodness rewarded . . . they have a precise elegance that's striking . . ."   —*Booklist*

Chosen as one of the "Ten Best Illustrated Children's Books of 1978."   —New York *Times*

"The telling here . . . is strong and will be accessible to young children and to reluctant readers who will appreciate the traditional theme of hidden goodness recognized and rewarded. The dozen paintings catch both drama and a somewhat Wyeth-like sense of the mysteriousness of open space."   —*School Library Journal*

THE LEGEND OF SCARFACE was Robert and Daniel San Souci's first picture book for children. Native Californians, the brothers have gone on to collaborate on other highly praised books for Doubleday, including *The Brave Little Tailor, Song of Sedna,* and, most recently, *The Legend of Sleepy Hollow.*

THE LEGEND OF
SCARFACE

A Blackfeet Indian Tale

ADAPTED BY ROBERT SAN SOUCI
ILLUSTRATED BY DANIEL SAN SOUCI

Doubleday
NEW YORK   LONDON   TORONTO   SYDNEY

Published by Doubleday, a division of Bantam Doubleday Dell Publishing Group, Inc., 666 Fifth Avenue, New York, New York 10103

Doubleday and the portrayal of an anchor with a dolphin are trademarks of Doubleday, a division of Bantam Doubleday Dell Publishing Group, Inc.

Library of Congress Cataloging in Publication Data
San Souci, Robert.
    The legend of Scarface.
    SUMMARY: A retelling of a Blackfeet Indian legend in which a young brave travels to the land of the Sun to ask for the hand of his beloved.
    1. Siksika Indians—Legends. [1. Siksika Indians—Legends. 2. Indians of North America—Legends]
I. San Souci, Daniel. II. Title.
E99.S54S16   [398.2] [E]

Library of Congress Catalog Card Number 77–15170
ISBN 0-385-13247-6 Trade
ISBN 0-385-13248-4 Prebound
ISBN 0-385-15874-2 Paperback
Text copyright © 1978 by Robert D. San Souci
Illustrations copyright © 1978 by Daniel San Souci
ALL RIGHTS RESERVED
PRINTED IN THE UNITED STATES OF AMERICA
9 8 7 6 5 4 3 2
9 8 7 6 5 4 3 2   (pbk.)

To All Native American Peoples

Many years ago, a boy lived among the Blackfeet Indians. He was called "Scarface" because he had been born with a mark on his cheek. His parents were dead, so he lived with his grandmother.

The other children of the tribe made fun of the boy because he was poor and because of the mark on his face.

Scarface spent much time in the forest and became a friend of the animals and birds; he even learned their speech. They were the brothers and sisters the boy had never known.

The chief of the tribe had a beautiful daughter named Singing Rains. All the young braves tried to win her affection, but she would have none of their boastful, arrogant ways.

Scarface, too, fell in love with her; but because he was poor and his face was scarred, he did not dare speak to her.

When the other braves found out that Scarface was in love, they made fun of him and said, "Since Singing Rains will have no part of us, maybe she will give her heart to one who is poor and ugly."

Goaded by what the others were saying, Scarface mustered his courage. One evening he spoke to Singing Rains beside the river.

The girl saw in him a generous heart and an honesty which the other young men did not possess. She did not see the scar at all.

She said to Scarface, "I would marry you. It doesn't matter that you are poor. My father would give us buffalo skins and horses. But I have made a promise to the Sun, who is the Father of us all, never to wed."

Scarface was saddened by her words and said, "You offer me joy, and then you take it away from me. Is there no way you can be freed from your vow?"

And Singing Rains answered, "If the Sun were to

release me from my promise, I would marry you gladly."

Scarface replied, "Then I will go to the Sun and ask this of him: for surely the Sun, who gives us all good things and is our Father, does not wish his children to be unhappy."

"How will you find the Lodge of the Sun?" asked Singing Rains. "Do you know the way there?"

"I only know that the Sun dwells beyond the Great Waters, which are themselves beyond the forest. Surely there will be those along the way who can guide me." So Scarface set out several days later to find the home of the Sun.

His grandmother, who loved him dearly, kept her tears in her heart until after their parting. She sewed him extra sets of moccasins and embroidered them with lucky signs made of porcupine quills. She prepared him a hide bag of pemmican made of pounded buffalo meat mixed with fat and berries.

It made Scarface sad to leave his home and his grandmother. The old woman waved to him until a turn in the path hid her from his view. But he set his face resolutely to the west, determined to find the

Great Waters and the dwelling place of the Sun.

When he had walked for many days, he came into a country where none of his tribe had ventured. Countless paths opened in front of him, and he was uncertain which way to go. The snows of winter were falling all around him.

While he paused, he spotted a wolf nearby.

Scarface called to the wolf, "Gray Brother, help me." Scarface had always been friendly with the animals of the woods, and the word of his kindness had spread widely.

The wolf came close and said, "You are Scarface, brother to us all. How may I help?"

"I am seeking the dwelling place of the Sun," he responded. "Can you show me the way?"

"I have never seen that place, but I am told that this trail will take you in the right direction." And the wolf indicated the left-most path.

So Scarface thanked the wolf and traveled on his way for several days.

Again he came to a place where the road forked, and he had to come to a halt. The snow was falling more rapidly now.

Spotting a mother bear and her cubs on their way to winter burrow, Scarface called out, "Sister, can you show me the way to the land where the Sun dwells?"

To her cubs, the she-bear said, "This is Scarface, who has shown kindness to our race."

To Scarface she said, "I have never seen the place of which you speak, but others of greater wisdom than mine have said that this path will carry one there."

With her paw she indicated which fork in the road he should take.

So Scarface thanked the she-bear and continued along the road she had pointed out.

After a long time, Scarface came to a place where the path disappeared completely. Snow was falling heavily all around. The land was still and white and empty: It seemed that neither man nor animal had passed this way before.

So he called to a pair of snowy owls who were watching him from a nearby tree, "Brother and Sister, can you show me the way to the Sun's home, which lies beyond the Great Waters?"

And the snowy owls told each other, "This is Scarface, of whom our cousins speak" (for word of kindness travels great distances, carried from heart to heart).

They answered the youth, "We have not seen the home of the Sun, but we have flown beyond the edge

of the forest to the shore of the Great Sea. Follow us, and we will take you that far."

So Scarface followed them beyond the edge of the forest to the shore of the sea.

And he thanked the birds for their assistance. When they had returned to the woods, Scarface stood alone, staring across the water.

There, in the far distance, he could see the faintest gleams, and he knew that that was where the Sun had his lodge. But how was he to cross such a great expanse of water?

Scarface spent three days and nights in prayer and fasting. On the morning of the fourth day, a pathway woven of mist and sunlight unrolled before him across the water toward the distant land.

Boldly he stepped out upon the path and ran along it as it wound ever onward, ever upward, for he felt that he was nearing the end of his quest.

When he reached the Land of the Sun in the sky, Scarface found another path stretching before him through a forest filled with the sweet perfume of growing things and alive with the song of birds, unseen in the thickly leaved trees.

The road underfoot was broad and flattened by the passage of many feet.

His heart was light as he walked along. He told himself, "Now, surely, the Sun, our Father, will not refuse my request."

He had gone only a short distance when he saw, resting against a tree trunk, a richly embroidered quiver. Though his heart desired this, he did not touch it, for he knew that it must belong to someone who would return for it.

A short time later, Scarface met a young man coming toward him. The young man was the handsomest person Scarface had ever seen. His clothes were decorated with beads, and his moccasins with brightly colored feathers.

"I have lost my quiver. Have you seen it?" the stranger asked Scarface.

"I have just seen it a little way back along the path. It is safe," Scarface answered.

"I am lucky you are an honest man," said the stranger. "A thief would have taken it, and it is the gift of my father." Then he asked, "What is your name? Where are you going?"

"My name is Scarface, and I am seeking the Lodge of the Sun, which I hope is very near, since I have been journeying a long time."

"My name is Morning Star, and the Sun is my father. Come with me while I reclaim my quiver, and I will take you to him."

So it was that Morning Star led Scarface to the Lodge of the Sun. It was huge and shining and painted with beautiful pictures which told the history of the world of men.

Morning Star introduced Scarface to his mother, the Moon, who wore a dress the color of the evening sky and earrings of gold.

She greeted Scarface warmly and invited him into the lodge and gave him food and water. She listened attentively while Morning Star told how they had met and Scarface told of his journey. But, out of shyness, Scarface hid the reason for his coming to the Lodge of the Sun.

When the Sun returned to his lodge in the early evening, he, too, greeted Scarface warmly. He praised him for his honesty and heard with interest the story of his travels.

Then the Sun invited Scarface to stay with them and refresh himself.

The Sun warned Scarface that neither he nor Morning Star should go near a certain mountain to the North, explaining, "Savage birds live there who will seek to slay Morning Star."

Scarface promised to stay away from that place, and he thanked the Sun and Moon for their kindness.

But in his heart he was troubled, and he asked himself, "How can I ask such a mighty lord as the Sun to release Singing Rains from her vow? Already he has extended me much kindness: to ask for more would surely seem ill-mannered and anger him."

So Scarface kept his secret sorrow to himself. For several days he followed Morning Star, who showed him the hidden pathways of the Sun's forest. Morning Star took him to a high peak from which Scarface could see below him the prairies and rivers and forests of the world of men, still in the hold of winter. Beyond, he saw the great sea, which in the distance climbed in a curve upward from blue to deep blue to purple to the rich black of night, and held in its substance all the stars of heaven the way a cobweb holds the dewdrops of early morning.

And the view both gladdened and saddened Scarface, for in all of its wonderful beauty he sensed the beauty of Singing Rains.

Now Morning Star had a secret wish to meet the savage birds and do battle with them, even though his father had forbidden it.

One day, while they were wandering through the forest, Morning Star slipped away from Scarface and went by secret paths to the northern mountain that was the home of the fearsome birds.

When Scarface discovered that his friend was missing, he immediately guessed where Morning Star had gone. So he, too, made his way to the distant mountain. But because he did not know the secret ways, he arrived long after Morning Star.

Scarface found Morning Star surrounded by the terrible birds, who screeched and slashed at the young man with their claws and beaks. They had him surrounded, and it seemed only a matter of time before they would kill him.

Heedless of his own safety, Scarface raced to his friend's side. His attack surprised the winged creatures and threw them into confusion. Taking this advantage, the two youths began to slay the birds, which did not retreat even when their companions sprawled lifeless on the ground.

When they had slain the last bird, Scarface and Morning Star rested for a time before they set off home again.

That night the Sun chided Morning Star for his disobedience and praised Scarface for his courage.

The Sun said, "This deed has earned you the right to ask a boon of me. What you wish, I will grant you."

But Scarface, still in awe before the Great Father, was unable to speak.

So the Moon stepped forward and said to her husband, "Though he remains silent, there are words in his heart which must be spoken, or his heart will burst trying to contain them."

Then, to Scarface, she said gently, "You are our son as surely as Morning Star. We will not deny you your heart's desire. Has not your father promised you this much?"

Moved by her kind words and manner, Scarface began, "Back in my village there is a maiden, Singing Rains, who has promised you that she will never wed. I ask you to release her from that vow, so that she will marry me, as she promised to do were she not bound by a sacred oath."

The Sun smiled and said to Scarface, "I release

the maiden from her vow. Return to her, Scarface, and claim her as your bride. Tell her it is my wish that she marry you. And this will be one sign of my will—"

Here the Sun touched Scarface upon the cheek, and the scar was gone. Then he handed the boy two raven's feathers and said, "Give these to the maiden as a further sign of my wish."

In the morning the Sun and Moon gave the boy rich clothes and many gifts and wished him well.

Then Morning Star led him to the edge of the sky land and showed him the shorter path home, which is called the Wolf Trail, or Milky Way.

Singing Rains saw Scarface coming from a great distance, and she ran out to meet him.

He handed her the two raven's feathers and told her that the Sun had released her from her vow and wished the two of them to marry. And he showed her where the Sun had touched his skin and healed the scar.

The people of the village marveled at his new clothing and the wonderful gifts the sky dwellers had given him.

The chief of the tribe greeted him warmly and welcomed the news of his daughter's wedding.

The young man was no longer joked about, but was honored by all the tribe.

He gave a portion of his new wealth to his grandmother, who greeted him with tears of joy. And he was called "Scarface" no longer, but "Smoothface."

He and Singing Rains were wed the following morning.

The Sun blessed the couple all the days of their lives, and the Moon gave them sweet dreams each night.